ZOOM AT SEA

by TIM WYNNE-JONES

pictures by ERIC BEDDOWS

A Laura Geringer Book
An Imprint of HarperCollins*Publishers*

Zoom at Sea Text copyright © 1983 by Tim Wynne-Jones. Illustrations copyright © 1983 by Ken Nutt. First published by Douglas & McIntyre, Toronto and Vancouver, Canada. Printed in the U.S.A. All rights reserved. Library of Congress Cataloging-in-Publication Data Wynne-Jones, Tim. Zoom at sea / by Tim Wynne-Jones ; pictures by Eric Beddows. p. cm. "A Laura Geringer book." Summary: Zoom the cat realizes his lifelong dream of nautical adventure in the home of a mysterious woman with magical powers. ISBN 0-06-021448-1. — ISBN 0-06-021449-X (lib. bdg.) [1. Cats—Fiction. 2. Magic—Fiction.] I. Beddows, Eric, date ill. II. Title. PZ7.W993Zo 1993 [E]—dc20 92-14738 CIP AC Typography by Christine Kettner 1 2 3 4 5 6 7 8 9 10 ❖ First American Edition, 1993

ZOOM LOVED WATER. Not to drink—he liked cream to drink—Zoom loved water to play with.

One night, when a leaky tap filled the kitchen sink, Zoom strapped wooden spoons to his feet with elastic bands and paddled in the water for hours. He loved it.

His friends shook their heads. "The sea is in his blood," they said.

The next night he made a boat from a wicker basket with a towel for a sail. Blown around the bathtub all night, he was as happy as could be.

"He comes from a long line of sailors," his friends whispered when they thought he was not listening.

Every night when other self-respecting cats were out mousing and howling at the moon, Zoom stayed indoors and sailed about in the dark. By day he watched the tap and dreamed.

"I'm at sea!" he said, twitching in his sleep.

Then, one afternoon while exploring the attic, he discovered a shelf he had not seen before. A dusty diary lay next to a photograph of a large yellow tomcat with white whiskers and a black sou'wester. Opening the diary, he found an inscription: "For Zoom from Uncle Roy."

Then he turned to the last page. There was an address and a map. "The sea and how to get there," it said.

The sea was not far, really. Zoom took a bus. He arrived very early in the morning at a house with a big front door. It was so early Zoom was afraid to knock, but the light was on and if he listened closely he thought he could hear someone inside. With great excitement he rapped three times.

The door opened. Before him stood a large woman in a blue dress. She wore silver earrings and many silver bracelets on her wrists.

Zoom cleared his throat nervously. "I want to go to sea," he said.

The woman smiled. "Speak up," she said.

Zoom put on his sailor's cap. "I'm Uncle Roy's nephew and I want to go to sea."

"That's better," said the woman, nodding. "Come in, my little sailor."

Inside, it was cold and damp.

"I am Maria," said the woman. "I'm not ready just yet."

The room was quiet and dark; everything was still. Far away Zoom could hear a sound like a leaky faucet.

He sat, trying to be patient, while Maria bustled around. Sometimes it was difficult to see her in the gloom, but he could hear the swish of her skirts and the tinkling of her bracelets.

The sea was nothing like Uncle Roy had described in his diary. Zoom was sure he had made a mistake and he was just about to sneak away when Maria looked at her watch and winked.

"Now I'm ready," she said.

And with that, she turned an enormous wheel several times to the right. The floor began to rumble and machinery began to whirr and hum. The room grew lighter and Zoom saw that it was very large.

Now Maria pushed a button and cranked a crank. Zoom could hear the sound of water rushing through the pipes. First there were only puddles but then it poured from the closets and lapped at his feet.

From rows upon rows of tiny doors Maria released sea gulls and sandpipers, pelicans and terns. From pots and cages she set free hundreds of crabs and octopi and squid who scurried this way and that across the sandy floor.

Maria laughed. Zoom laughed. This was more like it. Noise and sunlight and water, for now there was water everywhere!

Suddenly Zoom realized he could not even see the walls of this giant room, only the sun coming up like gold, and silver fish dancing on the waves. Through his eyeglass, far away in the distant blue, he spied a magnificent sailing ship. Maria said, "Go on. It's all yours."

Quickly he gathered some old logs and laced them together with seaweed. He made a raft and decorated it with shells as white as Maria's teeth.

When it was ready, he pushed and heaved with all his might and launched the raft into the waves.

"I'm at sea!" he said.

He danced around on his driftwood deck and occasionally cupped his paws and shouted very loudly back to Maria on the shore.

"More waves," or "More sun," or "More fish!"

Out he sailed, out into the distant blue. Waves crashed against the raft. The sun beat down. Fish leaped across the bow and frolicked in his wake. What a time it was!

Then the tide changed. The sea grew calm. Zoom scanned the horizon, but the sailing ship was gone.

He looked back toward the shore and saw Maria there. He realized that he was tired. He let the tide gently drift him back.

He sat with Maria at her long table drinking tea and eating fish fritters and watching the sun sink into the sea. As the light dimmed the room didn't seem half so big.

"The sailing ship I saw…" said Zoom.

"Your uncle Roy's boat," said Maria. "The Catship."

"So I just missed him," said Zoom sadly.

Maria's bun had come undone and there was sand in the ruffles at the bottom of her dress. Her jewelry tinkled silver in the twilight.

"He's bound for the North Pole," she said.

And then it was time for Zoom to go.

"Thank you for a great day," Zoom said. It had been perfect. Almost.

"My pleasure," said Maria. "Captain Roy will want to meet you."

Zoom was at the door. He turned. He could hardly believe his ears. "You mean I can come back?"

"Of course," said Maria. "When Roy returns. And he always does."

"Then so will I!" said Zoom.

"I'm sure you will," said Maria.

And he did.
But that's another tale.